THE WOLF HUNTER

Power, Religious Manipulation, and Contemporary Witchcraft

J.S RHIVBS

by
Joe Rhivbs

edited by
Moses Emorinke

Copyright 2020 Joe Rhivbs,
All rights reserved.

Published by eBookIt.com
http://www.eBookIt.com

ISBN-13: 978-1-4566-3566-4 (paperback)
ISBN-13: 978-1-4566-3567-1 (hard cover)

No part of this book may be reproduced in any form or by any electronic or mechanical means including information storage and retrieval systems, without permission in writing from the author. The only exception is by a reviewer, who may quote short excerpts in a review.

One of the toughest challenges the average Christian faces today is knowing what is real and what is not, because a lot of knowledge has been twisted.

False knowledge is gradually replacing true knowledge. And for those who haven't studied or researched this topic, the findings may surprise you.

The Wolf Hunter is based on the popular biblical verse:

"Beware of false prophets, who come to you in sheep's clothing, but inwardly are ravenous wolves."

—Matthew 7:15

Contents

THE MAJORITY 1

THE FALSE PREACHER 3

BUILDING THE EMPIRE, NOT THE SOUL 5

SELF-WORSHIP 7

ATTENDING CHURCH VS SEEKING GOD 9

NEEDS AND PROBLEMS FIRST, THEN SEEK GOD LATER? 11

THE MATERIAL CHRISTIAN 14

QUITE IRONIC ABOUT WHAT YOU BELIEVE 15

SOME THINGS CONTROL THE WORLD, AND THERE'S A REASON THE BELIEVER IS GIVEN A DIFFERENT SPIRIT..17

DO NOT CONFUSE POPULARITY WITH TRUTH 19

YOU CANNOT REPLACE GOD'S WORD WITH MOTIVATIONAL SPEAKING............................22

YOU CAN DEFLECT THE SPIRIT FROM ITS ORIGINAL SOURCE 23

MANY ARE NOT WHAT THEY THINK THEY ARE 26

ONLY THE SPIRITUAL CAN HEAR GOD........27

THE WAITING PERIOD 30

HYPOCRITES 31

FALSE HUMILITY...33

TRUTH WILL AUTOMATICALLY JUDGE LIES 34

THE BLESSING OF GOD IS NOT ATTACHED TO ANY MAN 35

WHY DO SOME TEACHERS OF FAITH CHALLENGE THE PROSPERITY GOSPEL? ..37

FIVE CHURCH STRATEGIES THAT AFFECT SPIRITUAL GROWTH 41

DEMONS, SO YOU THINK YOU KNOW THEM? 47

NO ONE CAN SERVE TWO MASTERS 49

THE SPIRIT OF THE DEVIL.............................50

CAN A BELIEVER BE CURSED? 52

"GOD'S PEOPLE" DOESN'T MEAN "CHURCH PEOPLE"..54

PUBLIC DISPLAY OF FALSE PERFECTION...56

THE BIBLE NEVER PRESENTED THESE TWO AS SUBSTITUTES 57

THE MAJORITY

A majority of churchgoers think that the size of the congregation defines how great a man of God is. A majority of churchgoers think that the number of miracles or signs displayed by a man signifies how close or how special a man is before God.

But a majority of churchgoers are wrong. People estimate greatness by how many people serve and honor them. But in the kingdom of God, greatness is measured by how we serve and honor others.

According to the Bible, whoever wants to be great among you, must be your servant. There is nowhere in the Bible that says that the size of a congregation, the weekly attendance, how many branches, or how much wealth a man has define how great a man is before God.

The Bible says that some prophesied and did wonders in my name, but I do not know them. But those who fed me when I was hungry, who clothed me when I was naked, those I know.

But unfortunately, many young ministers judge themselves by these false standards—void of the authentic gospel and more or less embedded in hell.

It's probably going to be hard to understand this, unless you can connect these verses

Whoever wants to become great among you must be your servant.

—Matthew 20:26

22 Many will say to me on that day, 'Lord, Lord, did we not prophesy in your name and in your name drive out demons and, in your name, perform many miracles?' 23 Then I will tell them plainly, 'I never knew you. Away from me, you evildoers!'

—Matthew 7:22-23

34 Then the King will say to those on his right, "Come, you who are blessed by my Father; take your inheritance, the kingdom prepared for you since the creation of the world. 35 For I was hungry and you gave me something to eat, I was thirsty and you gave me something to drink, I was a stranger and

you invited me in, 36 I needed clothes and you clothed me, I was sick and you looked after me, I was in prison and you came to visit me."40 Truly I tell you, whatever you did for one of the least of these brothers and sisters of mine, you did for me.

—Mathew 25:34-40

For the gate is narrow and the way is hard that leads to life, and those who find it are few.

—Matthew 7:14.

THE FALSE PREACHER

Beware of false prophets, who come to you in sheep's clothing but inwardly are ravenous wolves.

—Matthew 7:15

There is a difference between a preacher who is ignorant and a preacher with false intentions. A preacher who makes mistakes due to the fact that he is not as well informed or knowledgeable; this kind of preachers cannot really be referred to as a false preacher. His problem is just ignorance. But they're not really as dangerous as the false preacher.

The false preacher is not ignorant at all; he knows exactly what he's doing. He knows what he is doing is wrong, but he's intentionally doing it because of the gains it brings. You cannot really correct this kind of person because his problem is not a lack of knowledge. He may even know more than you.

Even if you approach him, he will know exactly what you're saying, and he may even feel sorry for you, and wonder why you don't like the benefits that come from his approach. In his situation, it is false personality and intention, not a lack of knowledge.

The only way you can tackle this is to address that personality and alert his victims. Because before one can get to that stage, that person must have made up his mind and killed his conscience.

BUILDING THE EMPIRE, NOT THE SOUL

He that winneth souls is wise.

—Proverbs 11:30.

The text does not say "he that winneth sovereigns is wise," though no doubt he thinks himself wise, and perhaps in a certain grovelling sense in these days of competition he must be so; but such wisdom is of the earth and ends with the earth. - C. H. Spurgeon.

Churches are getting larger, but not really affecting the world. That is because many care less about winning souls; they just want to build an Empire.

When you challenge a common way of reasoning, people don't like it. But we have to get to the point where we need to ask ourselves the question of what we want to define as church growth—whether by numbers or by spiritual growth. Because I don't understand how thousands of people can sit in a building, who don't even know the word of God. And then you say you have a growing church.

A drift from one church to another is not the same as soul winning. There isn't much soul winning happening anymore. All we have now is winning people to our churches. And what God says doesn't matter anymore, but what the leader says. Even when people join your churches, they are your best friends, and when they leave, they're your worst enemies.

What's the difference between that and a cult? When people give, and only the person they are giving to is the one getting richer, something is wrong. And any potential that God is using or that rises above the ceiling of the pastor or the general overseer gets cut down. That is nothing but pure witchcraft.

It is easy to think that you are winning souls to the kingdom of heaven, but you're just preparing them for hell.

Woe to you, teachers of the law and Pharisees, you hypocrites! You travel over land and sea to win a single convert, and when you have succeeded, you make them twice as much a child of hell as you are.

—Matthew 23:15

Enter through the narrow gate. For wide is the gate and broad is the road that leads to destruction, and many enter through it. 14 But small is the gate and narrow the road that leads to life, and only a few find it.

—Matthew 7:13-14

Solid food is for the mature, for those who have their powers of discernment trained by constant practice to distinguish good from evil.

—Hebrews 5:14

SELF-WORSHIP

But know this, that in the last days perilous times will come: For men will be lovers of themselves, lovers of money, boasters, proud, blasphemers, disobedient to parents, unthankful, unholy, unloving, unforgiving, slanderers, without self-control, brutal, despisers of good, 4 traitors, headstrong, haughty, lovers of pleasure rather than lovers of God.

—2 Timothy 3:1-4

There is a thin line between worshiping God and self-worship. Some things may sound and look like the gospel but may not really be it. Messages like "God loves you no matter what" are good. But the question is whether the people listening to this are listening to it because they have faith in God, or because it makes them feel good.

We have come to love messages that caress our ego and appeal to our selfish desires. But when messages talks about God and His principles, we don't like it, unless it's about us. We don't worship God anymore; we now worship ourselves.

You like the idea that God loves you no matter what you've done, but you cannot love God unless he does something for you. You like the idea that He loves you no matter who you are, but you cannot love others for who they are. You like the idea that God can forgive you, but you cannot forgive others.

You have completely taken God out of the pulpit and placed yourselves in it. 2 Timothy 3: 1-4 says, "In the last days men shall be lovers of themselves rather than God." You may not like the Bible, but it doesn't change the fact that most of its prophecies have come to pass. And it is so sad that this generation is fulfilling one right now.

For the time will come when they will not endure sound doctrine, but according to their own desires, because they have itching ears, they will heap up for themselves teachers; 4 and they will turn their ears away from the truth, and be turned aside to fables.

—2 Timothy 4:3-4

ATTENDING CHURCH VS SEEKING GOD

Grace comes through the knowledge of God. If grace is what you need, what else can I say to you?

> Grace and peace be multiplied to you through the knowledge of God and of Jesus our Lord.

—2 Peter 1:2

See, there's a big difference between seeking God and attending church. Just because you attend church, it doesn't necessarily make you a believer. And if you take your money to someone who tells you lies with the hope of winning a jackpot from God someday, it doesn't mean you're attending a church. It's more like a business center or a casino.

If it's all about the jackpot and not about God, then you will just be nothing but a gambler. It is in seeking God's knowledge and righteousness that we become a believer. It is also through His knowledge that we receive and sustain things that are given by God. You can attend a gathering inside a building and still not have knowledge of God, even though you call it a "church."

The building may be pretty, the building may be big, it may even be popular—and can still be a recruiting center for hell. What you call it doesn't matter. What matters is what they know and teach.

For I desire steadfast love and not sacrifice, the knowledge of God rather than burnt offerings.

—Hosea 6:6

Thus says the Lord: "Let not the wise man boast in his wisdom, let not the mighty man boast in his might, let not the rich man boast in his riches, but let him who boasts boast in this, that he understands and knows me, that I am the Lord who practices steadfast love, justice, and righteousness in the earth. For in these things I delight," declares the Lord.

—Jeremiah 9:23-24

NEEDS AND PROBLEMS FIRST, THEN SEEK GOD LATER?

You cannot tell the people to bring all their needs and problems first, then seek God later or even never. You and I know it doesn't work that way. With your show offs, you only make them more miserable.

"But seek first the kingdom of God and His righteousness, and all these things shall be added to you."

—Matt 6:33

The true word of God is the greatest miracle you can ever give to man. It doesn't throw fishes to you, but teaches you how to fish. And only through HIS words do we know him.

Just because someone told you that you wore a red dress yesterday and it happened that you wore a red dress yesterday, that makes them anointed men of God? If that's the case, spiritualists, psychics, and sorcerers should be called anointed men of God because they can sure tell you what you ate yesterday.

The Bible says seek ye first the kingdom of God, and every other thing shall be added. You cannot take the seeking part out and reduce the gospel to a show. Instead of sanctifying them with the word, you deceive them with show offs and baptize them with greed and self-centeredness.

Many will say to me on that day, "Lord, Lord, did we not prophesy in your name and in your name drive out demons and in your name perform many miracles?" Then I will tell them plainly, "I never knew you. Away from me, you evildoers."

—Mathew 7: 22- 23

Once when we were going to the place of prayer, we were met by a female slave who had a spirit by which she predicted the future. She earned a great deal of money for her owners by fortune-telling. She followed Paul and the rest of us, shouting, "These men are servants of the Most High God, who are telling you the way to be saved." \She kept this up for many days. Finally Paul became so annoyed that he turned around and said to the spirit, "In the name of Jesus Christ I command you to come out of her!" At that moment the spirit left her.

—Acts 16:16-18

Realize that it took Paul time to observe and discern this spirit. Demons can be misleading.

THE MATERIAL CHRISTIAN

Again, the devil took Him up on an exceedingly high mountain, and showed Him all the kingdoms of the world and their glory. And he said to Him, "All these things I will give You if You will fall down and worship me." Then Jesus said to him, "Away with you, Satan! For it is written, 'You shall worship the Lord your God, and Him only you shall serve.'"

—Matthew 4:8-10

The material Christian can only experience God under material conditions. The look and the size of the building, the side attractions that are available, and all the wealth that it promises to deliver. His sole objective is what he stands to gain in a relationship. So he approaches God with that concept, not knowing that it works the other way around.

Take away all the selfish desires from him and ask him to pray; he will be completely empty. You wonder why the devil promised Jesus all the wealth in the world, and Jesus didn't even give a damn? It's the same reason these people are fooled; the same strategy, no difference.

If you place material things before God, they have become an idol to you, and that's a fact. You think you are worshiping God, but there's an idol on that pulpit, and it controls the messenger. Though you cannot see it with your eyes, the messenger is loyal to his master.

Damn all your money and your many cars. Damn all your entourage, your mansions, and your jet planes. The true believer is above all these things.

QUITE IRONIC ABOUT WHAT YOU BELIEVE

If all blessings are from God, why does Proverbs tell us that the blessings of God make rich and add no sorrows? And why did the devil promise Jesus wealth on the mountain? Don't forget, Jesus was not in the club or some drug joint when Lucifer promised him wealth. He was praying.

But the carnal mind cannot understand this because his mind is carnal. And the material believer cannot understand it either because it doesn't know the word of God. He is deceived even in his prayers because he doesn't have what it takes to discern it.

Because his heart is filled with lust and many selfish desires, he will take any bait. He is brought up to recognize church by the items that are presented in the program. It doesn't matter if half of the church are backstabbing each other. As long as these items are presented well, to him it is church. He is conditioned by the choreography but void of the knowledge and righteousness of God.

SOME THINGS CONTROL THE WORLD, AND THERE'S A REASON THE BELIEVER IS GIVEN A DIFFERENT SPIRIT

In Your presence is fullness of joy;

—Psalm 16:11

The believer's spirit can be joyful in the presence of God. It does not need material possessions to be joyful or happy. The presence of God is enough to make it joyful. The spirit has the ability to emit full joy in the presence of God without any material possessions.

The more he comes closer to God, the more joyful he will be regardless of what is happening around him or what people are saying about him.

Nothing can make the believer's spirit more joyful than the way it is originally built. There is nothing wrong with material possessions. But you need to understand that the believer's spirit is unique and does not need material possessions to be happy or joyful. If these things will determine whether or not he should be joyful, it simply means that he wasn't truly transformed.

If he has it, that's not a problem. But a true believer will not use material possessions as a standard of success or reason to follow a messenger of God. That might be a standard for the world, but believers follow a different standard.

Though you have not seen him, you love him; and even though you do not see him now, you believe in him and are filled with an inexpressible and glorious joy.

—1 Peter 1:8

May the God of hope fill you with all joy and peace as you trust in him, so that you may overflow with hope by the power of the Holy Spirit.

—Romans 15:13

For the kingdom of God is not a matter of eating and drinking, but of righteousness, peace and joy in the Holy Spirit.

—Romans 14:17

DO NOT CONFUSE POPULARITY WITH TRUTH

So we only know about the last three years of Jesus's ministry and his childhood. We don't know much about his life in his teenage years, nor in his twenties. But the question is—where did he spend those years, and from whom did he learn?

He sure didn't learn from those materialistic priests in the temple. He didn't talk like them, he didn't look like them, he didn't dress like them. Though he preached on the mountains, his knowledge was different and far more superior than those priests in the temple.

You do not need a pulpit to be validated for doing God's work. As long as you can reach people and impact them in many ways, that's what matters. A big congregation is not the measure of a successful church.

Jesus fellowshipped with only 12 and affected over 20 billion people. Some have many followers who can't even affect their neighbors, thereby producing fake Christians whose ignorance is becoming an obstacle in their environment.

Do not seek after any preacher who delights in the ignorance of his followers, reaping them of everything. It is your responsibility to seek and search for the truth, and the truth shall make you free.

7 In vain do they worship me, teaching as doctrines the commandments of men.

8 You leave the commandment of God and hold to the tradition of men.

9 And he said to them, "You have a fine way of rejecting the commandment of God in order to establish your tradition!"

—Mark 7:7-9

But when he, the Spirit of truth, comes, he will guide you into all the truth. He will not speak on his own; he will speak only what he hears, and he will tell you what is yet to come.

—John 16:13

And ye shall know the truth, and the truth shall make you free.

—John 8:32

"All truth passes through three stages. First, it is ridiculed. Second, it is violently opposed. Third, it is accepted as being self-evident." - Arthur Schopenhauer

The Italian astronomer, Galileo, was ridiculed for saying the earth revolves around the sun. He was charged with heresy, a crime for which people were sometimes sentenced to death, simply because they confused 'Popular' with 'True.' Jesus was charged for challenging the popular teachings of the scribes and Pharisees. His ideas were considered as a threat to the popular teachings of those held in high esteem. But Christ was authentic. Truth will judge a hypocrite; therefore he will not allow it. So it's the responsibility of the seeker to search for it. So let's re-examine the premise by which we validate a successful ministry. Jesus' ministry was not even in church, it

was outside church. Yet he had more impact.

YOU CANNOT REPLACE GOD'S WORD WITH MOTIVATIONAL SPEAKING

You cannot replace God's word with motivational speaking. It is by the spirit that we connect to God, and this is something that a motivational speaker will never understand.

It is also by the spirit that we receive, discern and understand the things of God. A messenger of God speaks with the Spirit of God, and he is not ashamed of the one that sent him. He comes to the altar to exalt God before you, and not your feelings, ego or your endless desires.

His sole purpose is to make you have faith in God and not in any other thing or anyone else.

Hebrews 11: 6 says that "But without faith it is impossible to please God. For he that must come to God must believe that God exists and that He is a rewarder of those that diligently seek him." Let me remind you that the faith that the Bible is talking about here is the faith in God and not in anyone or in anything else.

90% of the people who go to church now don't even know the word of God. You cannot preach the word of God and take God out of the equation.

A gift may be from God, but that doesn't mean that all gifts are used on behalf of God. God gives everyone life, but some people do whatever they like with their lives. They may have the intellect, but they do not have the spirit.

YOU CAN DEFLECT THE SPIRIT FROM ITS ORIGINAL SOURCE

A believer must grow in order to reach his full potential because his spirit is not necessarily replaced but reborn. He does not grow by the number of activities or the number of years spent in church. He grows in the knowledge and understanding of the word. No amount of motivation can grow his spirit.

The spirit operates differently and more powerfully than the one he was originally born with. It has the ability to fight supernaturally, even when the believer is held to a stalemate physically or mentally. It is the power propeller of the believer.

But if you can deflect the spirit from its original source, which is the word, you may be able to render the believer useless such that any demon can use his head as a broomstick.

The effect of his prayers is also minimal because his spirit is weak. Do not confuse activities for progress or spiritual growth. The spirit can only grow by the word of God.

That He would grant you, according to the riches of His glory, to be strengthened with power through His Spirit in the inner man.

—Ephesians 3:16

For God has not given us a spirit of timidity, but of power and love and discipline.

—2 Timothy 1:7

Like newborn babies, long for the pure milk of the word, so that by it you may grow in respect to salvation.

—-1 Peter 2:2

But grow in the grace and knowledge of our Lord and Savior Jesus Christ. To him be glory both now and forever! Amen.

-—2 Peter 3:18

But the seed on good soil stands for those with a noble and good heart, who hear the word, retain it, and by persevering produce a crop.

—-Luke 8:15

So that you may live a life worthy of the Lord and please him in every way: bearing fruit in every good work, growing in the knowledge of God.

-—Colossians 1:10

MANY ARE NOT WHAT THEY THINK THEY ARE

When people pray collectively in a nation and nothing is happening, that shows the prayer's collective power. It means so many are not what they think they are. And if they think they are, someone is either teaching them wrongly or deceiving them.

See, I've heard this before —that there is power in prayer and even men of God have powers. And that can be misleading. You see, you can pray in the flesh and still not get results because the only power is in the presence of God.

The Bible says without faith, it is impossible to please God, which means two people can pray to God and still not have the same results even though they're both praying the same prayers. If the power is in the act itself, then everyone should have the same results.

The Holy Spirit connects us into the realm of the spirit, because only in the spirit are the things of God real. If the things of God aren't as real as they used to be to you, then you must have quenched the spirit, because faith makes a lot o the difference.

The preacher may tell you that he saw a mountain in front of you. But there is no mountain except your ignorance. A man's ignorance is his mountain. You may drink of the anointing oil, pray as much as he tells you; you may even lie down on the floor and let him march all over you, but without faith, you still cannot please God.

The Bible says that my people perish for lack of knowledge.

ONLY THE SPIRITUAL CAN HEAR GOD

As much as we like to talk about Christ, many forget that prayer was a big part of his life. As a matter of fact, it was the activity he did the most.

If you understand prayer the way you should, you would realize that any way is a way. Either way, you win. It is difficult for anyone to work against you if you know how to pray because the things that are meant to work against you still end up working in your favor.

In the spirit, there are no limited dimensions. The way up could be down, and the way down could be up. But we live in a world where everyone feels entitled to everything, and it is possible to bring this attitude into faith.

Because faith is not just believing God for something, there are responsibilities involved. Until you do what you must do, you cannot get results. For everything Jesus did, he spent time preparing, praying and listening to his Father. Because the instruction is where the result is.

But only the spiritual can hear God because God is a spirit and those who worship him must worship him in truth and in spirit.

It's noted that He sometimes prayed all night long. In the garden of Gethsemane, the Bible states that He sweated blood, so great was His conversation with His

Father. He specifically withdrew to a solitary place to avoid being distracted by others. Maintaining a focus on God is the main idea so that we can hear Him speak to us in return. An attitude of prayer means that we are very much aware of the presence of God and that He is always listening. Don't be afraid of what anyone is doing to you or saying about you. You will still be where God wants you to be. You cannot choose the way of the spirit—he chooses the way.

And it came to pass in those days, that he went out into a mountain to pray, and continued all night in prayer to God.

—Luke 6:12

For God is Spirit, so those who worship him must worship in spirit and in truth.

—John 4:24

And we know that all things work together for good to those who love God, to those who are the called according to His purpose.

—Romans 8:28

THE WAITING PERIOD

Until the time came to fulfill his dreams, the Lord tested Joseph's character

—Psalm 105:19

Jesus was told that his friend Lazarus was sick, and he didn't even show up until three days later. And when he finally got there he said, "Father, I thank you because you heard me." Many people misinterpret this event as a break.

But what was he doing in those three days? And why was he thanking God? If all that you are looking at in this event is a miracle, you may totally miss the whole essence of that event because the revelation is not in the fact that he raised Lazarus from death, but what he said in the few moments before he raised him. He said, "Father I thank you because you heard me."

This only shows to you that there is a waiting period in prayer and that he had been praying to God until that day.

There is a waiting period. In the book of Acts, the apostles had to wait ten days before the spirit came. They prayed for ten days.

Depending on the situation, the waiting period may be different. But you have to continue praying through that period. There is God's time. And what he gives you is perfect.

It was nearly 14 years between Joseph's dream and the time he left prison to become second in command of Egypt. It was nearly 15 years between the time David was anointed king and actually became king. It took a total of 25 years for the promise of God to Abraham to be fulfilled. THIS PATTERN IS FOUND ALL THROUGHOUT THE BIBLE.

HYPOCRITES

Hyp·o·crite (Noun) William Webster's Dictionary.

1: a person who puts on a false appearance of virtue or religion.

2: a person who acts in contradiction to his or her stated beliefs or feelings.

I can understand why a short person might be offended when you say something bad about short people. They were born that way. The same goes for all genders, colours, or anyone born with a distinct difference from others.

What I do not understand is why when you speak out against hypocrisy, even without mentioning names, some people get offended.

It just shows you how much they have come to accept it as their identity, and it is so sad that some members of the church have also come to accept this identity, such that when you talk about a hypocrite, they think that you are insulting their entire tribe.

It is important to know that not everyone in the church that went through a conversion experience is truly converted. Some were either born, grew up in the church or are infused into the church through certain participation.

Therefore, these kinds of people approach it like a tribe, but not necessarily like ones who were truly converted.

It doesn't matter how you are infused into the church; the fact is that you still need to be converted in order to see the things of God the way they truly are.

FALSE HUMILITY

Humility can mostly be measured through intentions and not necessarily the action displayed, so it's hard for many to know. False humility is one of the strongest tools to scam a religious person.

Some false prophets intentionally display acts of humility as an art of seduction.

The scam is usually made to appear real, presenting the victims with what they like and admire when in fact, it's just a tool to distract the victim from the very intention; it's called the art of seduction and the devil uses this. It's a working scam because your victims may never see it coming.

You cannot judge by sight who is really humble. That's why discernment is very important for all believers. Because not everyone who hugs even in church truly loves you. On the inside, they might just be snakes.

To test all spirits, whether they're of God means to discern beyond the actions especially, when it looks too good or too perfect to be true.

TRUTH WILL AUTOMATICALLY JUDGE LIES

Truth will judge lies whether you intend to judge it or not. Those who reverend religion over God's words, and His righteousness have automatically placed themselves in the other side of truth because religion is a lie, and the word of God is true.

We cannot stop lies from feeling judged when the truth comes. We cannot stop darkness from disappearing when the light comes.

Let us all worship God who has given us instructions by His words and not religion because religion is man-made, and they are all lies. Religion does not represent the body of Christ. Even Christ attacked religion.

Just because you are defending religion doesn't mean that you are defending the body of Christ. And if you leave a place because you are not growing spiritually, it doesn't mean that you have left the body of Christ, because one church cannot represent the whole body of Christ.

THE BLESSING OF GOD IS NOT ATTACHED TO ANY MAN

But seek first his kingdom and his righteousness, and all these things will be given to you as well.

—Matthew 6:33

Although the Bible mentions a number of wealthy individuals, the richest person by far was King Solomon. Interestingly enough, he did not ask for wealth.

The blessing of God is not attached to any man but to His will and righteousness. Even when you fall and hands are laid on you, you will come back again and fall again. But the main goal of God's blessing is to retain.

Falling does not necessarily translate into a blessing. Neither is it a truest sign that you have received the spirit of God. Any spirit can knock you down or predict your future.

The Bible is written like a puzzle. You read in one place, "seek ye first the kingdom of God, and every other thing shall be added," and then, you read in another place, "whatever you ask you shall be given." Please understand that one is hanging on the other.

If you think that they contradict, it is because you haven't figured out the puzzle. God didn't bless Solomon with wealth because Solomon asked for wealth. He blessed him with wealth because Solomon asked for knowledge and wisdom. Solomon was wealthy, and he didn't ask for it.

Having the knowledge and righteousness of God is the most effective route to God's blessings. Whatever objects, materials or selfish desires, they're baiting you with, do not take the bait.

If only you can cultivate the discipline to shift your focus away from whatever object, material, show offs or selfish desires they're baiting you with, and focus on seeking knowledge and righteousness, you will see how your life will go. Do not take bait; the more you do, the more you will be distracted and held down.

Moreover, I WILL GIVE YOU WHAT YOU HAVE NOT ASKED FOR—both wealth and honor—so that in your lifetime you will have no equal among kings.

—1 Kings 3:13

WHY DO SOME TEACHERS OF FAITH CHALLENGE THE PROSPERITY GOSPEL?

So, from the Old Testament to the New Testament, there is this chronological establishment that if you trust in God's grace and providence, you shall be blessed. In that, if you follow the commands of God, you shall prosper.

Even Jesus said that—seek ye first the kingdom of God, and every other thing shall be added. So, are there prosperity messages in the Bible? Yes, there are prosperity messages in the Bible. Is there something wrong with preaching a prosperity message? No, there's nothing wrong with preaching a prosperity message.

So, the question is, why do some teachers of faith challenge the prosperity gospel? The prosperity gospel was actually pioneered by a man named Oral Roberts. The gospel presents the view that if you follow God's command, great things will happen to you in a material sense.

There are others that learned from Mr. Roberts and later turned it into a "fact" that what God is actually requesting from you is material things like tithings, offerings, first fruits, etc. And that these are like the major things God is really concerned about. Every other thing is minor. If you are not giving these things, you cannot possibly be blessed.

Even though we don't understand the word of Christ, or we don't even understand the Bible, we should be able to understand the story of Job because it is presented as a story.

We know that Job was a perfectly righteous man according to the Bible, but yet, Job still suffered losses. And Job's friends came to him and said, "You must have done something wrong to God." And Job inquired of the Lord, "What is it that I did wrong?" And God said, "You did nothing to me."

So, according to the Bible, we also know that Job's losses had nothing to do with what he did wrong. Don't forget that the kind of losses Job suffered, not many Christian could suffer those losses without backsliding.

But we know that Job's loss did not have anything to do with what he was giving or what he was not giving to God. It seems that modern prosperity gospel tends to align with what Job's friends were told, Job rather than what God told Job.

The idea that we serve God for material blessings is what is destroying a lot of people's relationship with God today. It's craziness to claim that a man's possession are a way by which we can measure God's endorsement of a man or how much God loves him.

I think these are sick ideas. Know that Job loved God, despite his losses. Despite those things, Job continued to love God. He continued to be loyal to God, and God even blessed him the more. People like Solomon are among the wealthiest of all time. Solomon was actually the wealthiest man that walked with God, and he man didn't even have a need to ask for wealth.

It is as simple as this—if you are loyal to God, if you are continuously loving in your relationship with God, you will be blessed, no matter what.

Job's losses or gains have nothing to do with what he did wrong or what he did not give to God. God gave back all his

losses because he continued to be loyal to him despite all his losses.

And everyone who has left houses or brothers or sisters or father or mother or children or farms for My name's sake, will receive many times as much, and will inherit eternal life.

—Matthew 19:29

FIVE CHURCH STRATEGIES THAT AFFECT SPIRITUAL GROWTH

Some took to logic wisdom to fulfill their ambitions, and it's starting to backfire, while many will carry on their carnal legacy. We don't have many churches anymore, but rather, religious corporations. There is such thing as knowledge of good and knowledge of evil; both can be effective in their own ways, for their own goals, but not all wisdom is of God.

I preach a relationship between God and man and not between church and man, and this may make me unpopular among religionists.

What I'm revealing today has nothing to do with whether this strategy works or not. It has a lot to do about the spiritual effect of these strategies or whether they align with the knowledge of God.

(1) Fear of the leader: The idea behind this strategy is that people can be controlled by fear as it will successfully prevent unwanted behaviors coming from lack of appreciation. Most dictators adopt this strategy. Gang leaders, cult organizations, religious leaders, and even slave masters adopt this strategy.

Political philosophers, like Machiavelli, made this strategy popular. The strategy suggests that while it is wonderful for a leader to be loved, it is most effective for him to be feared, as human nature is somewhat ungrateful and will continue to ask for more and expect the leader to meet unrealistic needs.

Therefore, a leader needs to display characteristics that will make people not question his authority. And this fear should be used in a way that is justified so that it doesn't create hatred among followers, since followers tend to side with the most persuasive arguments. When you see some religious leaders emphasizing their ability to curse or ruin the lives of any of their followers that don't fall in line, this is the strategy they are using.

But when you look at Proverbs 9, it says that the fear of God is the beginning of wisdom, which means that the fear of God should be the core Foundation of God's wisdom—not the fear of Man.

(2) Consequences over truth: Consequences of an action rather than the sincerity of intention or truth of a matter.

One of the reasons why many people that seek power keep a lot of secrets is because they believe that the consequences of an action should outweigh the truth of a matter or the sincerity of intentions. In other words, it should be about the consequences of an action, not the sincerity of intention or the truth—since consequences tend to bring in more effects.

In other words, if we say that tithing is voluntary, what are the consequences of that action, what are the consequences of that truth, what are the consequences of that intention? Even if the intention is sincere, even if it is the truth of the matter. Most power seekers believe that the consequences should outweigh such truth. In other words, it shouldn't be revealed. Such truth should not be revealed.

Some of the followers share the same ideology. These followers believe that it should be about the consequences of an action, not actually the truth of a matter or the intentions behind what you're saying. You're going to hear these followers say things like, "Don't preach something like this because it is going to discourage people from coming to church; it is going to discourage people from giving; it is going to discourage people from this and from that." If you listen to them talk, you will realize that they share the same ideology with these power seekers.

These followers also believe that the truth ought to be concealed if the consequences do not favour a particular ambition. Even though the knowledge of God says that God judges' intentions rather than actions but these people turn the scriptures all around

(3) Status over spiritual maturity: The idea behind this strategy is that when you put people that are richer, or people that have a higher status, in a position of leadership, they will tend to finance the work of God, they will attract their kind, and the group may also have access to their resources and connections.

While this strategy may bring you the numbers, money, and resources, it can also backfire, because it tends to put people that are spiritually ignorant in charge. And in turn, these people produce spiritually ignorant people like themselves, who know nothing about the word of God,. They know a lot about corporate formation but they lack the knowledge of God.

(4) Traditions over Christ: Church traditions over the word of Christ. Some ambitious church leaders believe that in order to successfully build a brand, the church traditions should be more emphasized than the word of Christ. This will make the members uncomfortable to worship anywhere else outside that tradition. But what happens is that these members begin to use the church traditions as the authentic measure of the knowledge of God or the work of God.

If you read the book of Mark, it says that you have rendered the word of God ineffective by your traditions. Even Jesus addressed this. But some church leaders ignore things like this. In order to build a brand, they go for this. One of the effects of this is also that many of the branch leaders will tend to now rely on the brand rather than the knowledge of God itself.

(5) Using carnal means to attract or persuade: I'm not even talking about decorations of churches or any of that. I'm talking about things like auctioning miracles, telling people that if they want blessings from God, or if they want some miracle, they can put a certain amount down (or if they don't have that amount, they can put another amount down), and the auction goes on and on. There are no spiritual foundations for such an approach. That is just pure logic.

DEMONS, SO YOU THINK YOU KNOW THEM?

I was first mentored by an exorcist specialist before I moved on to my teaching call. And I learned that not all evil spirits are violent. And not all who are influenced by evil spirits put on a circus show. Although I've seen all manner of shocking behavior from the victims, they are much more advanced than what a lot of people think.

And what I am doing I will continue to do, in order to undermine the claim of those who would like to claim that in their boasted mission they work on the same terms as we do. For such men are false apostles, deceitful workmen, disguising themselves as apostles of Christ. And no wonder, for even

> Satan disguises himself as an angel of light. So it is no surprise if his servants, also, disguise themselves as servants of righteousness. Their end will correspond to their deeds.
>
> —2 Corinthians 11:12-1

Demons are fallen angels. When they fall, it doesn't mean that they have lost their abilities. Demons or angels, like seraphims, can heal, and are known for their healing powers. While the cherubs, who also can heal too but are specially known for their knowledge gifts.

Unlike man, their knowledge is not limited to what is happening before them. They have knowledge of the past, present and future. Due to man's curious nature, they are usually the most sought-after. And surprisingly, the devil is in the category of these spirits.

But unlike men, both angels and demons can network without talking. If you interact with one demon, all others can access that communication. If one demon possesses a body, all others can know what that demon knows. And if one angel falls, all other angels can know that one has fallen.

It is important to judge all spirits whether they are truly of God. Be careful of whom you're talking about your life to, or whom you are seeking the past or the future from—unless you want to make your life a database for demons.

There are s many things you don't understand, and that's the reason why Jesus and his disciples were more concerned about you having the knowledge of God before any other thing. Be careful of the multiple gods you worship. Be careful of whose messenger you're consulting. For there is only one God whose sole intention is to love you and has no need to bait you.

NO ONE CAN SERVE TWO MASTERS

No one can serve two masters; for either he will hate the one and love the other, or else he will be loyal to the one and despise the other. You cannot serve God and mammon

—Matthew 6:24

Jesus never compared any spirit with God except mammon. He referred to both as masters. To compare with means to point out differences in objects regarded essentially as of the same order.

Mammon is a spirit or an entity that promises wealth through greedy pursuits of gain. Jesus said you cannot serve mammon and God. Virtue is not compatible with greed.

Yes, it is true that God wants His children to prosper, but the idea that we only need God to get material possessions means that money is the very God, and God is just another medium.

This is not true prosperity. It is just another perverted form of worship.

THE SPIRIT OF THE DEVIL

There is only one spirit that asks people to worship and sacrifice to him in exchange for riches and glory. And that spirit is not the spirit of God—it's the spirit of the devil.

In Matthew 4:9, he asked Jesus in the wilderness to bow down and worship him in exchange for riches and glory. There are many spirits that are more brutal and violent than the devil. But the spirit called Satan is a knowledge spirit. Rather more subtle and diabolical in his approach, he lures his victims through ignorance, especially by offering some form of reward.

One of his unique abilities is to lure and tempt his victims through ignorance. It's really rare to see him fighting and rolling his victims on the floor. There are other demons that are known for that. He's a knowledge spirit and he understands his strength. If you can understand the nature of this spirit, you might be able to tell how he operates.

But God is most known to demand his knowledge and righteousness, and His blessings are without sorrows. Those who bring you the true knowledge of God bring you a weapon to overcome the devil. The knowledge of God is still the most effective weapon against this spirit.

When he met with the Christ on the mountain, rather than being violent, he tested his knowledge of God, and then tried to make a deal with him. When he met with Adam in Eden, he took advantage of his ignorance and told him what he would gain if he did the opposite. (Matthew 4:9) "All this I will give You," he said, "If You will fall down and worship me."

CAN A BELIEVER BE CURSED?

One of the first things you have to know is that curses no longer have the right to operate in your life. It doesn't matter where the curses are coming from, whether your enemies, friends, parents, pastor or general overseer.

There is therefore now no condemnation to those who are in Christ Jesus, who do not walk according to the flesh, but according to the Spirit. For the law of the Spirit of life in Christ Jesus has made me free from the law of sin and death.

—Romans 8:1-2

Can believers curse those who persecute them?

Bless those who persecute you; bless and do not curse them.

—Romans 12:14

Believers are instructed not to curse people that persecute them or that disagree with them. Even Jesus prayed for his accusers.

Are pastors and general overseers exempted? Can they curse you or curse people that disagree with them? The answer is also no. God cannot empower something that he doesn't support. If he says do not curse, it also means he will not give power to it when you curse. A general overseer title means nothing to God. It may mean something to you, but it means nothing to God. According to the Bible, God honors his words, not titles. It is impossible for God to support someone who is manipulating his words, or ignorant of his words, over the person who is speaking his words in truth, simply he is in a more prestigious position, or has a more impressive title.

You also can't curse someone that God has not cursed.

> How shall I curse, whom God hath not cursed? Or how shall I defy, whom the Lord hath not defied?
>
> —Numbers 23:8

This behavior is mostly common with preachers that are obsessed with power and self-glory. But the fact is, that is unethical and it's wrong.

"GOD'S PEOPLE" DOESN'T MEAN "CHURCH PEOPLE"

> God is a Spirit: and they that worship him must worship him in spirit and in truth.
>
> —John 4:24

When you hear terms like "God's people," it doesn't necessarily mean "church people." Rather, it refers to people who worship God in truth and in spirit, and people like this may be found anywhere. Many of God's people also go to church, but not all church people are close to God. Not even everyone who opens a church is a true messenger of God. While some actually lead a house of God, some just lead business centers. To some, it's about taking advantage of their congregation. But that is not God's way of righteousness.

When you're in a group of dishonest people, the one that is honest will be seen as someone who lacks wisdom because they believe embracing dishonesty is what is safe and what works in that group. But what works in one place or realm may not work in another. Don't mistake the Kingdom of God with a group of greedy and dishonest people who think that the deluded results they have in their churches count before God.

If you look at some animals, like a dog for example, they're very wonderful creatures in terms of respect for closeness. If a dog lives with you, it may be stronger than you, but that dog will not take advantage of that superior strength towards you. In terms of such feelings, he is quite higher than a human. Because not many humans can do that, but he is a creation of God, and God is even higher than that. He respects closeness too, and you'll be amazed at some of the things he can do for your sake.

PUBLIC DISPLAY OF FALSE PERFECTION

Christ was great before God, yet so simple. You don't have to act perfectly to be righteous. When you're truly something, there is no need to prove it.

They say that the real wealthy people are the least dressed in the room because they have nothing to prove to anyone. And those who make a big show of their money and cars have something to prove.

It may even surprise you that couples that hold hands and kiss every two minutes in public may likely be the ones that fight the most.

When you see a Christian with so much display of false perfection, you should be suspicious. Because if you're truly it, there will be no need to always prove it.

You don't need to put on public displays of false perfection to please God. Neither do you worship God for other people's approval.

THE BIBLE NEVER PRESENTED THESE TWO AS SUBSTITUTES

There are two theological extremes out there about praying. There are those who think that all we need to do is pray, and that taking action means you have no faith.

Then there's the other extreme—the theology that if we can do things by our own power, we don't even need to pray at all.

But the Bible never presented these two as substitutes. As much as the Bible encourages us to take action, it encourages us to pray as well.

If praying wasn't important, Jesus wouldn't have done it. But it was the most important thing he did, and I'll tell you why.

Only those who see praying as a means to taking something for themselves fall for these two extremes.

But those who approach it as a relationship will hardly fall for these theologies because communication is an important factor in any relationship.

Take away communication from a relationship you have ended that relationship. As much as Jesus preached, he was always looking for every opportunity to talk to the Father, which shows you how close they are.

It sounds ridiculous for someone to claim that he or she is trying to build your relationship with God by advising you to stop talking God. That's theology from hell.

The Bible never said you shouldn't do anything yourself, but it says talk to God about everything, which includes the things you can do by yourself.

Compiled by Moses Emorinke

Cover design by Michael Josephs

CPSIA information can be obtained
at www.ICGtesting.com
Printed in the USA
BVHW011759021120
592331BV00001B/3

9 781456 635671